JUDY MOODY AND FRIENDS
Jessica Finch
in Pig Trouble

Megan McDonald
illustrated by Erwin Madrid
based on the characters
created by Peter H. Reynolds

CANDLEWICK PRESS

For Ashley
M. M.

For my nieces, Melanie and Mariel
E. M.

Adopting a pig—or any pet—is a big decision. Make sure you understand the time, care, and cost involved before making a final commitment and bringing any critters home! If you are interested in learning more about owning and caring for potbellied pigs, ask your local librarian to recommend an authoritative and reputable guide, or search online for more information.

Text copyright © 2014 by Megan McDonald
Illustrations copyright © 2014 by Peter H. Reynolds
Judy Moody font copyright © 2003 by Peter H. Reynolds

Judy Moody®. Judy Moody is a registered trademark of Candlewick Press, Inc.

First edition 2014

Library of Congress Catalog Card Number 2012947726
ISBN 978-0-7636-5718-5 (hardcover)
ISBN 978-0-7636-7027-6 (paperback)

15 16 17 18 19 CCP 10 9 8 7 6 5

Printed in Shenzhen, Guangdong, China

This book was typeset in ITC Stone Informal.
The illustrations were created digitally.

Candlewick Press
99 Dover Street
Somerville, Massachusetts 02144

visit us at www.candlewick.com

CONTENTS

CHAPTER 1
Just Say *Oink*

Pigs, pigs, and more pigs! Jessica
Finch loved pigs.

Jessica Finch had a dream. A big
pig dream. She dreamed of having a
pet pig.

If she had a pig, they would read
books together. And ride bikes. And
have sleepovers.

Jessica called her friend Judy Moody. "Emergency," she told Judy. "Come right away."

Judy Moody rode her bike up the hill to Jessica's house.

"I came as fast as I could," said Judy. "What's the emergency?"

"It's a pig emergency," said Jessica Finch.

"RARE!" Judy said.

"Come on," said Jessica, and Judy
followed her upstairs to her room.

Jessica's room was pink. Pink, pinker, pinkest. Pinker than bubble gum. Pink as a pig's tail. And her room was full of . . . pigs. Pig books. Pig pillows. Pig posters. Piggy banks. Even a fuzzy piggy-face rug.

"Your room is one big pigpen!" said Judy.

"Thanks!" said Jessica. She glanced out into the hall. She closed her door. She made her voice almost a whisper.

"Okay. So. You know how it's almost my birthday, right?"

"Right! Happy *almost* birthday," said Judy.

"And you know how there's only one thing I want for my birthday, right? More than anything else in the whole world."

"Umm . . . a piggy cake?" asked Judy.

"No. Not a piggy cake.

Not a piggy coin purse.

Not a piggy clock.

Just one single present. A real-live,
cute-as-a-button, potbellied pig."

Judy's eyes grew as big as gum balls.

"Potbellied pigs are super cute and super smart and super cuddly," said Jessica. "And I dropped a million and one hints, like telling my parents that my birthday just happens to be on the same day as National *Pig* Day."

"Really?"

"Really."

"Happy *almost* Pig Day, too," said Judy. "But I think you have about a million in one chance of getting a real live P-I-G. You might as well ask for an aardwolf."

"A-A-R-D-W-O-L-F," said Jessica Finch, Super Speller.

"So what's the emergency anyway?" Judy asked.

"Right. You have to help me snoop around. I just have to know if I'm getting a P-I-G."

"Judy Moody, Super Snoop, at your service. Where do we start?"

Jessica squinted her eyes. Jessica pinched up her face, thinking. "I know!" she said. "Under my mom and dad's bed."

"You think there might be a pig under your mom and dad's bed?" Judy asked.

Jessica Finch snorted. "No, see, we snoop for normal presents. If we find any, that's bad. If we don't find any, that's good."

Judy scrunched up her face. "How is *no* presents a good thing?"

"If we don't find presents, I just know I'm getting a real pig. If we find normal presents, no pig."

Judy just shrugged. She had no pig sense at all.

"Come on. I know all the good hiding places," said Jessica. "You be my lookout."

"Roger," said Judy.

"Who's Roger?"

"Never mind," said Judy.

"If you hear footsteps, just say *oink*," Jessica told Judy. "One oink for Mom. Two oinks for Dad."

"Gotcha," said Judy.

Jessica took Judy's arm and dragged her down the hall.

Jessica looked under the bed.

Jessica looked in
the window seat.

Jessica went to
look in the closet.

13

"Oink! Oink!" Judy was oinking!

"Who? What? Where?" asked Jessica.

"I think I heard footsteps," said Judy.

Jessica listened at the top of the stairs. Quiet. Dead quiet. "I don't hear anything," she said.

"Sorry," said Judy. "False-alarm oink."

Jessica opened the closet door. She stood on a box. She pulled down a bag. *Crunch, crunch, crunch* went the paper. Jessica's heart sank.

"Oh, no!"

"What's wrong?" Judy asked.

"I found presents," said Jessica.

She peered into the bag. "A piggy
flashlight. An I ♥ Piggies notebook.
Even a game called Pig Out. That
means no potbellied pig."

"Oink," said Judy.

"Ratday," said Jessica, slumping
down on the bed.

"Huh?"

"It's Latin. Pig Latin for *drat*."

CHAPTER 2
This Little Piggy

Jessica Finch was ummedbay outway. B-U-M-M-E-D O-U-T.

Judy tried to cheer her up. "Let's play the game," Judy whispered.

"What game?"

"The Pig Out game!" said Judy.

"Now? But it's for my birthday. My mom will get mad."

"We'll just play it once," said Judy. "C'mon. It'll be upersay unfay."

"Super fun! Then we put it back and nobody will know?" said Jessica.

"They don't call me Super Snoop for nothing," said Judy.

Jessica perked up. She ran back inside, grabbed the game, and then ran back to her room.

In no time, Jessica and Judy sat crisscross applesauce on the fuzzy pink piggy rug.

"So, how do you play?" asked Judy.

Jessica tore the lid off of the box. "There's no board. You just roll the five little piggies like dice," said Jessica Finch, Pig Expert. "And you get points for how they land." She showed Judy the score chart.

Judy rolled the pigs. "Snorter! Ten points!"

Jessica rolled the pigs. "Side of bacon! Minus ten points!"

Judy rolled the pigs again.

One landed on top of another.

"Pig pyramid!" yelled Jessica. "Is that good?"

"Good? That's fifty points!" said Jessica. "You win."

"Play again?" Judy begged.

"Shh," said Jessica. "Did you hear that?"

"Hear what?"

Somebody was coming up the stairs.

"Quick! Hide the pigs!" Jessica whispered.

Judy shoved the pigs under the rug. Jessica hid the box under her bed.

Mrs. Finch walked past Jessica's room. Mrs. Finch went down the hall into the bathroom.

"Phew. That was close," said Jessica.
"I better put this back."

"And I better go home," said Judy.
"Before we get in *pig* trouble."

Jessica and Judy laughed like hyenas.

"Are you sure you have to go?"

"Yep. I have to feed the . . . um . . .
my Venus flytrap."

As soon as Judy was gone, Jessica put the game back in the box. "One little, two little, three little, four little piggies—" Uh-oh! Piggy Number Five was issingmay! Missing!

Jessica looked under her leg. She looked under the rug.

She looked under the bed.

NTBF! Nowhere To Be Found. Pig-a-ma-jig!

Jessica Finch ran out of the house and hopped on her super-pink bike. She rode super fast to Judy Moody's house. She honked her Super Pig bike horn all the way up the driveway to the Moody backyard.

Jessica took off her helmet. She heard noises coming from a blue tent in the backyard. A tent with a sign that said T. P. CLUB.

"Knock, knock," called Jessica.

Judy poked her head out of the tent flap.

"Do you know where my pig is?" Jessica asked Judy.

Judy's eyes bugged out. "Pig? What pig?"

"One of the little plastic piggies is missing. From the Pig Out game."

"Oh, *that* pig," said Judy.

Pee! Gee! Wee! Gee!

Jessica heard a strange sound. She looked around. "Hey, what was that sound?"

"What sound? I didn't hear a sound."

Pee! Gee! Wee! Gee!

"There it is again. A squeak. A high-pitched squeak."

"Maybe it was a mouse," said Judy.

"It was louder than a mouse."

"I mean, maybe it was Mouse. My cat."

"Your cat's in there?"

"Sure. Why not?"

Jessica shrugged. Then she heard the sound again.

Pee! Gee! Wee! Gee!

"There. Didn't you hear *that*?"

"Squeaky door," said Judy.

"But your tent doesn't have a door," said Jessica. Sometimes Judy Moody was one oink short of a litter.

"Then it must be Stink," said Judy. "Squeaky Stink."

"Your little brother's in there, too?"

"Sure. Why not?"

"Well, can I come in?" said Jessica.

"NO!" said Judy. "I mean, no."

Stink popped his head out of the tent, too. He pointed to the word *CLUB* on the sign. "Members only," he said.

"Yeah, sorry. Those are the rules," said Judy.

"But I never get to be in your clubs. Can't I be in your club? Just this once? For my birthday?"

Judy shook her head. "Rules are rules," she said.

"Atray inkfay," said Jessica.

"I am not a rat fink," said Judy.

Jessica Finch made a pinch face. Jessica Finch felt like she might cry.

"Judy Moody, you are not a friend. You are not even a Super Snoop. You are just . . . a big . . .

M-E-A-N-I-E!"

Jessica Finch stomped away. She stomped across the grass. She stomped down the sidewalk. She hopped on her bike and sped all the way home. She did not look back once.

"MOM!" she yelled when she got back home.

"Kitchen," her mom called.

"Judy Moody is my UN-friend. She is UN-invited to my parties."

"But, honey, you already asked her," said her mom.

"Then I will UN-ask her."

D-R-A-T! National Pig Day was about to become National Rat Day.

CHAPTER 3
The PeeGee WeeGee Club

At last it was March first. Jessica Finch's birthday. National Pig Day! The only thing missing was one perfect pet potbellied pig.

Jessica Finch had not one, but two parties: an after-school piggy party and a next-Sunday bowling party. Jessica Finch had a piggy cake and pink ice cream with her friends Rocky, Frank, and Amy Namey. NOT with Judy Moody.

Jessica Finch opened piggy presents.

Jessica Finch and her friends played Pig Out—minus one piggy.

"Happy Birthday!" said Amy.

"You don't seem very happy," said Frank.

"Yeah, why are you such a Debbie Downer today?" asked Rocky.

Just then, Jessica Finch heard a sound. A high-pitched squealing sound—*Pee! Gee! Wee! Gee!*—coming from right outside her very own house!

"It's that sound again!" Jessica said. "You guys hear that, right?"

"What sound?" said Rocky and Frank at the same time.

"I don't hear anything," said Amy,
but she couldn't help giggling.

Jessica ran down the hall. *Was she out of her peegee-weegee mind?*

She ran to the front door. She peeked out the window. *Judy Moody?*

"Go away, Udyjay Oodymay!" she called.

"Just open the door," said Rocky and Frank.

"Yes, just open the door," said Amy.

Jessica Finch crossed her arms. Jessica Finch turned her back to her friends.

Jessica Finch did not open the door.

"Jessica, open the door," said her mom.

"Let Judy in," said her dad.

Rat fink! Even her parents were being pig heads.

Jessica Finch cracked open the door. "I'm still mad at you," she told Judy through the crack.

Pee! Gee! Wee! Gee!

There it was again. That sound! Louder than ever!

Jessica Finch flung open the door.

There was Judy, holding a lumpy
yellow baby blanket in her arms. And
curled up in the lumpy yellow baby
blanket was . . . a cute-as-a-button,
perfect, potbellied piglet!

It had fuzzy pink legs, fuzzy gray
polka-dot spots, and a curly pink tail.

It even had a big pink bow tied
around its head.

"*Pee! Gee! Wee! Gee!*" went the piggy.

Jessica Finch squealed and jumped
up and down.

Judy handed over the squirmy bundle of pig. "He's from your mom and dad," she said.

"Happy Birthday, honey," said her parents at the same time.

Jessica Finch could not believe her eyes. Jessica Finch could not believe her ears, arms, or elbows.

"Thank you, thank you, thank you, Mom and Dad," said Jessica. "But how? Where? I looked everywhere. When did you—"

"He was hiding at *my* house!" squealed Judy.

"We asked Judy to take care of the little guy for a few days," said Jessica's mom.

"Judy Moody, Pig Sitter, at your service," said Judy.

"Ohh! That's why you wouldn't let me in the tent!" said Jessica.

"Sorry I acted like a weenie," Judy said.

"Sorry I called you a meanie," Jessica said.

"Pee! Gee! Wee! Gee!" said the little piglet.

Jessica A. Finch's very own
potbellied pig.

"He's perfect!" she said.

"I know. Let's have a piggy party!"

Jessica and her friends played
with the new piggy. They fed him
baby cereal . . .

and goat's milk.

They played with a squeaky toy,

a ball,

and a stuffed cat.

"What are you going to name him?" asked Jessica's mom.

"How about Mr. Piggles," said Amy.

"Oinkers," said Judy.

"Sir Squeals-a-Lot," said Frank.

"Norman Vincent Pig," said Rocky.

Jessica needed a perfect name for the most perfect pig in all the world.

"Pee! Gee! Wee! Gee!" said the pig.

"I'm going to name you PeeGee WeeGee," said Jessica. "And I'm starting a new club. The PeeGee WeeGee Club!"

"Uh-oh," said Judy.

"Uh-oh is right," said Frank. He wiped his hands down the sides of his pants. "What do we have to do to be in the club?"

"You just have to be able to say *PeeGee WeeGee!*" said Jessica.

"PEEGEE WEEGEE!" everybody shouted.

PeeGee WeeGee curled his tail right around Jessica's little pinky finger.

"He curled his tail!" said Jessica. "I bet that means he's happy."

If Jessica had a pig tail, she would have curled it, too. Jessica A. Finch was in Pig Heaven!